A Donkey Named Flea

Written by Mark Phillips

Illustrated by Chris Sushynski

PUBLISHING
12

This is Flea.

His full name is Flea Bitten Donkey, but he prefers Flea.

His master called him that every day. "Get up, you Flea Bitten Donkey! Carry that load! Oh, you are a useless beast!"

Flea was a nice donkey, but he did not like to work very hard. Whenever he got a chance, he would sit down. This would enrage his master who would whip him and yank on his reins.

Flea did not much care for his master.

Imagine Flea's delight when he learned he was being sold to someone new! The man was going on a trip and wanted a donkey to go with him.

"I will make a terrific traveling buddy, as long as I do not have to work too hard and I get enough time to rest."

His new owner introduced him to a woman.

"This is my wife, Mary," he said.

"Hello! My name is Flea!" the donkey said.

"Oh Joseph," Mary said, "I think he's hungry." She gave him a carrot.

Joseph took sacks of food and supplies and loaded them onto Flea's back. Flea stood patiently, but he was beginning to wonder how much he would be expected to carry. When all the bags were loaded, Flea sighed in relief. That was about as much as he wanted.

Then Joseph lifted Mary onto Flea's back.

Flea began to worry about this whole trip...

They walked for what seemed like forever that first day. Flea didn't complain because he didn't want his new master to whip him as his old one had done. However, he was very tired before long, and Joseph would not let him rest.

They traveled for days and days. Flea's hooves hurt and he was always thirsty. Once, he saw a small creek and ran over to get a drink. He was still drinking when Joseph yanked on his reins.

"What are we going to do with you?" Joseph asked.

"Let me take a break!" Flea said.

Soon they were back on the road.

One day, they came to a river. Joseph began to lead Flea into the rushing water. "No, no!" Flea hollered. "I am scared of water! I can't swim! I don't like cold and wet! Don't make me go!"

He dug his hooves in and wouldn't budge an inch.

"Please donkey," Mary said. "I need you to carry me across."

Joseph pulled and Mary begged and eventually they got Flea across.

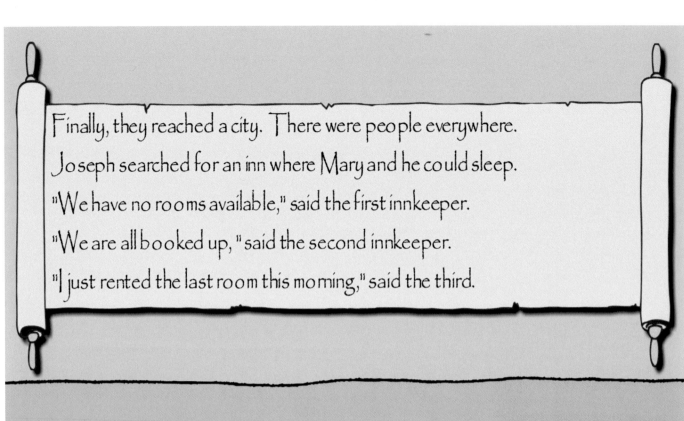

Finally, they reached a city. There were people everywhere.

Joseph searched for an inn where Mary and he could sleep.

"We have no rooms available," said the first innkeeper.

"We are all booked up," said the second innkeeper.

"I just rented the last room this morning," said the third.

By now, Flea was exhausted. He could not go another step, not a single step. When Joseph came out of the fourth inn, again looking disappointed, Flea fell to the ground and would not be moved.

"Donkey!" Joseph snapped. "We must keep going!"

"Joseph!" Mary yelled. "The baby..."

Joseph carried Mary to another inn.

"Please," he said to the innkeeper, "My wife is about to have a baby. We need a place to stay."

The innkeeper said, "I am so sorry. We even have people sleeping in the kitchen. The best I have is a stable. It is warm and dry, if you don't mind the smell."

"We'll take it!"

Flea watched as Joseph and Mary disappeared around the corner. He waited until he had enough energy to move on. Slowly, he stood and followed them. He saw a water trough and went over to get a drink. He took a nibble from a nearby juniper tree. Finally, he found the couple in a stable behind the inn.

What he found with them made his mouth fall open. There in Mary's arms was the most beautiful baby Flea had ever seen. His eyes were so bright, they seemed to light the entire night; his smile held the love of God Almighty; his soft cooing filled Flea with a peace and joy he had never felt before.

Flea wanted nothing else but to be near this baby.

Soon men came to the stable. Some brought sheep. Others brought gifts. All of them bowed down to the baby. How important he must be! "His name is Jesus," Mary told their visitors.

Eventually the family was left alone. Joseph, Mary, and the baby fell asleep in each others' arms. Flea stayed awake, staring at the scene. He knew he had to stay with these special people, no matter what.

Joseph awoke with a start. He woke Mary up and they began to speak
intently. What was the problem? Flea wondered.

"We have to go now!" Joseph whispered.

"But we need to rest," Mary said, both being cafeful not to wake the baby.

Go? Flea worried. Would they take him with them? Now that Mary had delivered the baby, would they still need him? He knew he hadn't been as helpful as he could have been on their trip. He comlained a little. He didn't obey as much as he should. What would he do if they left him here? He knew he never wanted to let Jesus out of his sight again. He would do whatever it took. He prayed that God would let them understand how much he needed to be with them.

He opened his mouth to plead his case when Joseph spoke.

"The angel in my dream said, 'Take Mary and the child and *flee* to Egypt.'"

Thank you Lord! Flea thought, they're taking me with them!

Joseph put Mary and Jesus on Flea's back and the four of them quickly left the city and went to Egypt.

From that day on, Flea became the hardest working donkey in the
Middle East. Joseph never had to ask him twice to do any chore or carry
any load. His favorite job, however, was carrying Jesus on his back.
In fact, once Jesus was an adult, Flea carried him in a parade into Jerusalem.

But that is another story.

DraW NeW adventures For Flea!

Made in the USA
San Bernardino,
CA

58772270R00015